COMMERCIAL FICTION

DAVE HOUSLEY

Outpost19 | San Francisco
outpost19.com

Published 2013 by Outpost19.

Housley, Dave
      Commercial Fiction/ Dave Housley
      ISBN 9781937402600 (pbk)
      ISBN 9781937402617 (ebook)

Library of Congress Control Number: 2013917422

OUTPOST
19

PROVOCATIVE READING
SAN FRANCISCO
NEW YORK
OUTPOST19.COM

These stories originally appeared in the journal *Hobart.* Many thanks to editor Aaron Burch.

Cialis

"How did you even get these tubs out here?" I ask.

He squeezes my hand. "It's a secret," he says. "Happy anniversary."

I reach across the space between our tubs and dip a fingertip into the soapy water, wiggle it toward his nether region. "Is it working yet?"

He looks down. Can he really not tell without looking down? Getting older is full of surprises, almost none of them welcome. "Not yet," he says.

I rub a soapy hand across my thigh and look out over the lake. How he got the resort people to put these tubs out here, I have no idea. I know they weren't here yesterday, when we had drinks at the fountain that stands maybe thirty yards to the right. I know they weren't here this afternoon, when we had lunch on the restaurant's terrace. I know they were sitting on the top of the lake's bank, steaming and soapy and ready to go, when we donned swimsuits and robes and headed down to what I thought was going to be the hot tub.

It is lovely, though: the manicured lawn trailing down to the lakefront, dark green water giving way in the distance to the mountains speckled with Fall. An Ansel Adams morphing into a Jackson Pollock. A couple walks past us. They glance and look away. I sit up, hoping they can see the band of my swimsuit.

"For god's sake, William," I say. "People think we're naked under here."

"But we're clearly wearing swimsuits," he says, shooting the last word out toward the fountain.

The man nods his head and the woman giggles. I scrunch further down under my bubbles.

"This is lovely," he says. He looks at me and smiles. There are years on his face. History. But I can still see the glint in his eye, the mischievous smile, the confidence that made me wait for him in the hallway after Freshman Comp some forty years ago. Now I know, of course, that confidence can be a tricky thing. Confidence can mean time shares and junk bonds, tech start-ups and sub-prime mortgages. Confidence can get you sitting out on the lawn of a five star resort in a lukewarm tub waiting for an erection that may or may not come.

My water is starting to get cold and my hands are wrinkling. We've been out here for an hour and I'm starting to wonder about logistics. "How did they get hot water out here anyway?" I say. "Did people have to carry these things? Is this a normal thing that they do? Was it extra? Did you tip them?"

"So many questions," he says. "Can't you just appreciate this?"

"Wouldn't one tub have been a little more, you know, efficient?" I say. I try to put a smile into my voice, a flirt. I like to think that I can still make that appendage rise without the help of pharmaceuticals.

2

"Maybe you could just appreciate the gesture," he says. He looks out over the lake and sighs. "On the question of a single tub. May I remind you that I'm a partner. There's a certain…I mean, we couldn't just… *do it right here in the middle of the Greenbriar*." He stage whispers the last part and I'm immediately overcome by the melancholy that's been stabbing at me lately. Menopause or something else, I'm not sure.

"So on a practical level," I say. "When that pill starts working, are we just going to walk back to the room like nothing is happening. There are people playing shuffleboard over there. They're starting karaoke at the bar."

He shakes his head, stares out over the lake. He wipes a hand on the side of the tub, picks up his iPhone.

"Mr. Romantic is checking his email," I say.

"Can't you just…" he starts. A young couple walks over to the fountain. They are holding hands. The man puts his hands on the woman's leg and whispers in her ear. They giggle. He sits down and she leans over onto his lap, gazing up at the clouds. They look like they have all the time in the world. "I think it's starting to work," he says.

"You think?"

"Actually," he says. "Not yet."The sun is setting over the ridge and the sky purples. Karaoke sounds trickle down from the bar, a woman doing a capable version of *My Way*.

"Should we have dinner brought in?" I say. "Or would you like to go to the restaurant again?"

My water has gone cold and goosebumps are form-ing on my thighs.

"Hold on," he says, "this will start working soon."

Wrangler

"I thought you were going to play football," she says.

"Yeah," I say.

"You're wearing jeans."

"Yes."

She is folding laundry, matching socks. She rolls a pair into a neat ball and drops them into the basket. Even for this, she has a system. She has equipment—a thirty dollar "Laundry Pal" from Crate and Barrel. She rolls and drops, rolls and drops.

I pull up my pants and reach into the Sears bag for the new socks—black, UnderArmour. I noticed this last week. Brett wears the jeans, and then athletic socks and the Nikes. But the socks are black, so they go better with the jeans. I had just normal socks on last week, the white ones like we wore in high school basketball. I had it wrong.

"Wait," she says. "I've never seen those jeans before. Those are like Mom jeans. Those are like Eighties jeans."

I can feel the heat rising to my cheeks. My forehead sweats. I look at the socks, take a deep breath. Do I want to get in a fight? I glance at the clock radio. It's 2:30 and it will take twenty minutes to get over to the athletic fields. Game starts in an hour. Last week he didn't arrive until right around three, a half-hour early, making some joke about old habits dying hard. This week, he could be there earlier. He could be there right now, standing around, wondering why there's nobody to throw to.

I decide to go the direct route. "You know what these are, Sally," I say.

"Really?" she says. There's a little bit of laughter in her voice, a little bit of pity. "Those are *Wranglers?*"

I nod.

"Turn around," she says.

I feel ridiculous but I do it.

"Huh," she says. "They took that W thing off them. But those are Wranglers alright."

There are a million things I could say, like how can you notice one pair of new jeans but not when I shaved my mustache or when I lost twelve pounds on that South Beach Diet, like how can somebody who buys hundred dollar jeans six at a time on the internet make any comments about anybody else's jeans?

I remember what the marriage counselor said. "Yep," I say. "Wranglers all right."

I put on the new sneakers. Cross Trainers. Nike. Almost the exact kind that Dale Junior wears when he comes out. Close to the same kind, but not too close. It's tricky. It's a line we're all trying to walk. It's nothing we would ever talk about, not ever, but I see the rest of the guys doing the same thing, all of us slowly picking up on it, morphing, figuring it out—Wranglers and Nikes and black UnderArmour socks and dark green and mustard colors.

You can take it too far, though. Last week, Earl Tucker from the Legion had on the exact same non-branded, Packers-colored shirt that Brett had on the week before. The same one. I wanted to ask if he had Googled it, or just got lucky at the Sears. It was too much, though, a step over that line. Brett would never say anything, but he didn't throw a single ball Tucker's way all afternoon, and when we were hanging out by the pick-ups afterwards, Brett and Dale joshing and slapping each other on the shoulders and the cameras getting every moment of it, Tucker was not asked to "come on over and have a few."

Sally finishes with the socks and starts in on her underwear—white cotton, sensible, the kind you picture on your mother but not your wife. She folds each one the same way, right over the center, left over the center, bottom over top, and into the Laundry Pal for the five-step trip to the dresser.

"Do they all wear those?" she says. "To play in, I mean? You do, like, play football?" She's trying to be neutral, to really ask the question, show interest. This is a thing from the marriage counselor and she's not very good at it, but I appreciate it so much I want to cry or punch the television.

What did the counselor say? Communicate. Be honest. Be friends again, then let the lovers part come back on its own. She said all that and then she wrote the prescription for the little blue pills and asked about the co-pay.

"Well it's not really a real game," I say. "I mean, it is a real game, but…" How can I explain it so she'll understand? Do I want her to understand? Do I want to think about it enough, even, to be able to explain to somebody else?

I take the belt out of the Sears bag. This is another thing I had wrong. You don't wear your work belt to play football on Sunday afternoon with Brett Favre and Dale Earnhardt, Junior. I feel like maybe somebody should have told me that, but the main rule seems to be that we don't talk about it any more than to say something like, "you coming out Sunday?" Like any of us would miss it. Like we're not counting days until we can be out there again. Like we're not holding our breath hoping he doesn't lose interest or get signed by some playoff team with a gimpy quarterback and then what would Sundays be again but the day before we slog back to work?

"But it's football," she says. "In jeans?"

Communicate. Be honest. Be friends again. "Yeah," I say. "They do all wear them. Dale Junior, too, when he comes. It's not bad. I mean, if you do get tackled or you fall down or something, you know, there's enough fabric there to..." I feel like I'm ten years old, trying to explain Batman to a grown-up.

"You don't have to make it make sense, Tom." She says it softly, puts a hand on my arm. "I get it."

I squeeze Sally's hand. It's warm and a little moist. She smells like Fabreeze. "Thanks," I say. I want to tell her everything, how effortless it looks when he throws the ball, how amazing it feels to catch one of those spirals, what it's like after we play, when we're leaning against the trucks and cracking jokes, listening to Brett tell stories about Lambeau Field or the Super Bowl, how it feels like we're in the center of the world all of the sudden, like the cameras amplify everything—the jokes, the game, the jeans, the Nikes, even my own little life. I want to say all of that but it's getting late and Sally has moved on to her jeans and I picture him there, standing next to the pickup with a bag full of footballs and wondering why he even bothers with this shitty little town and us assistant managers and sales reps and teachers and accountants.

"Hey," I say, "I really gotta get going."

Budweiser

The man woke up and walked to the bathroom. He relieved his bladder and looked at himself in the mirror. He looked at the clock. 6:25. He could either go back to sleep or head down to the basement to do P90X. If he waited until later, there was a chance he would forget or, more likely, would be too tired to even change into his workout clothes. He crawled back in to bed and got under the covers. He would try to do P90X in the afternoon, maybe even at lunch. For right now, there was a warm bed.

Boy, he thought, I sure do miss that horse.

•

The man boiled spaghetti and opened a can of tomato sauce. Organic. A full dollar fifty more than the usual kind. He wondered if he would even notice. He wondered if it was too late to be thinking about making that kind of a switch. He had grown up on antibiotics and pesticides, Cheez Whiz and Pop-Tarts and Oscar Mayer wieners.

He wondered what that horse was doing now, how his foot hair was coming along. He had tried to groom it, but had never had much luck. And there must be a better word for it than foot hair, right? Surely the Budweiser people knew. This was another difference between them, an example. He took out the notebook that he kept in the back of his pocket, the one labeled REASONS. "I don't even know what that foot hair is called and I bet they do," he wrote.

•

The man turned on the television. The Three Stooges. Curly hit Moe in the back with a frying pan. Funny, the man thought, how much it looks like assault with a deadly weapon now. He remembered a thing the horse used to do, pushing at his back while the man was readying his oats. That was some horse, he thought. On the television, Larry and Moe floundered in a swimming pool while Curley paddled a little canoe around the periphery, dropping rocks on top of them.

•

The man sat down at Chili's and ordered a cheeseburger. He had forgotten to bring a newspaper or a book. He thought about going outside to get a paper, a free weekly, real estate listings, whatever, but he worried that the waitress would think he was running out on the tab. He read the placemat. "Wild West Nachos!!!" it read. There was a picture of a cowboy and a horse.

The waitress came to fill his Coke and the man shook his head and smiled like he and the waitress were in on some kind of joke. She ignored him, filled his Coke, and clacked away toward the bar.

The man checked his phone but there weren't any messages. He ate half his cheeseburger and went to the bathroom. When he came back, the waitress stopped by to ask him if everything was okay. "I tell you what…" he said.

"Everything okay, sir?" the waitress asked, raising her voice.

He pointed to the placemat. "Reminds me of this horse," he said. "One I was training for the Budweiser people. The Clydesdales."

"Our beef is one hundred percent grade A certified angus," the waitress said. She sounded like she was reading something off a cue card. "You want to talk to the manager that's him over there."

"Oh no," the man said. "I just mean this picture. Reminds me of this horse."

"You let me know if you need another refill on that Coke," she said.

•

The man had a beer and read the newspaper. There was a story about the Clydesdales coming to a nearby city. "Well I'll be," he said.

He drank three more beers and took the empties out to the barn. He set the bottles in a row and gathered some rocks into his pockets. He wound up like a baseball pitcher and threw. He knocked over the first bottle and danced a little jig. "Not bad, huh?" he said. He turned to the stable, but then he remembered that it was empty.

He knocked over the rest of the bottles, one by

one, and then went back inside.

•

The man went to the tax place in the mall. The tax preparer was a young guy, Latino, wearing Dockers and a tie. "So you haven't worked for a full year?" he said.

The man nodded. You could really hear the guy's accent, he thought, when he said the word "year."

"The last time you worked was for...Bud-weiser?"

"I was training this horse," the man said.

"A year ago then?" the tax guy said. "Nothing in this last tax year?"

"He was a pretty cool horse," the man said.

The tax guy nodded, tapped something into his computer. The printer started to whirr. "We're all set here," he said.

•

The man went to see the Clydesdales in the nearby city. There was some kind of parade. He wasn't sure what it was for, or why there'd been an article about it in the paper, but he was happy to have something to do. He was happy that he might have a chance to see the horse again.

He wondered if he'd recognize the horse. He wondered if the horse would recognize him. But then he reminded himself that the horse was a horse.

He took a spot on the street near a family with twin girls in matching dresses and pigtails. Every now and then somebody threw candy from a float and the girls would skitter across the street to gather up lollipops or Tootsie Rolls. He ate popcorn from a paper cone. He drank a Coke. He watched marching bands and politicians he didn't know riding by in classic cars. They waved and he fought the polite urge to wave back.

Finally, the Clydesdales came into view. He was pretty sure he knew which one was the horse. If he was right, they had definitely done a better job with that foot hair stuff, whatever it was called. The horse looked bigger. Businesslike, if that made any sense. The horse looked like a Clydesdale.

The man watched the Clydesdales pass. A fire truck came along next. Then a few more marching bands. His feet were getting sore. He thought about the drive home. He found his pickup, paid for his parking, and made his way along the crowded city streets. He made a right onto the Eisenhower Expressway and watched the city roll by in his window. So many people. From Eisenhower he got on 88 West and the traffic loosened up. He increased his speed. He was looking forward to getting home. That was some horse, he thought.

McDonald's

We pull into the campground and it's just like I imagined it would be: chaparral scrub receding to oaks and firs as we move up into the mountains on a gently winding road. You'd never know we're only an hour outside Los Angeles, the traffic and the smoke and the crowds. I look around the car at Josh and Tommy and Laurel, all of them beautiful and cool and careless in that way that only beautiful people who know they're cool can be, like they chose the clothes they're wearing by accident, forgot to brush their hair, rolled out of bed and into the car, and still wound up looking like they just walked out of an Abercrombie and Fitch catalog.

If being Laurel's little sister has taught me anything, it's that I don't look like this, that I'm not and will never be one of these people.

I watch Josh and Tommy watching her. They've probably forgotten that I'm even sitting here, next to Josh, behind Tommy, diagonal to Laurel and her jean shorts and a top that I've never even seen before and her blond hair cascading in the wind. She twists in the seat to adjust her shorts and Tommy nearly drives off the road into a sign that says "Welcome to Angeles National Forest."

"Almost here," Tommy says.

"Are those guys meeting us?" Josh asks.

"They were getting the party supplies," Laurel

says. She says the last few words like they're the password to some magical kingdom and I picture some kind of velvet curtain rolling back to reveal everything I've been missing so far in my first sixteen years. This is what Laurel's been doing while I've been studying. I'm a muggle and she's Harry Potter, queen of this world that I couldn't even see until today. Of course, I knew it all along, or I suspected. There's always been something about Laurel that's been untouchable, unseeable, a part of her that she keeps just for herself. This, here, in the car with her and Tommy and Josh on our way to something they haven't even seen fit to tell me about yet, is as close as I've ever been.

"Who brought the shoes?" Laurel says. "You guys get the shoes?"

"In the trunk," Tommy says. Then he adds, "Southwest Regional Semi-professional Hamburger and Sodapop League Champion." He says it like it's a joke and it's not a joke, like he's hedging his bets on which it is to Laurel.

"Damn straight," she says. "Burger and Soda League horseshoe champeen. That's me." Tommy and Josh laugh. Tommy pushes at her shoulder. "Undefeated," Laurel says, and I wonder what the hell they're talking about, why they think it's so funny. Could they really be talking about horseshoes? Hamburgers? As usual, Laurel says everything like there's some part of it that we'll never understand, some part she's saving for somebody who isn't here yet.

"You ready, little sister?" Tommy says. In the

rearview, his teeth are straight and white. His hair looks like it was tousled by the most highly paid Hollywood stylists. He looks like a guy in a band on a made for television movie.

"My name is Brenda," I say.

He nods. His eyes move back toward the road. "Right," he says. "Brenda."

"Whooooose mix is this?" Laurel asks. There's a crackle to her voice, a flirt that I'm not used to hearing.

Tommy sits up in his seat. "Um…" he says.

"This song is soooo good, you guys!" Laurel says. She turns in her seat, holds her fist out and Tommy does the same. They bump. "Dave Matthews Band are the bomb, y'all," she says.

"Y'all?" I say. "Since when do you say 'y'all,' Laurel?"

She shakes her head and sighs.

"DMB!" Tommy shouts out the window.

The three of them sing along: "*aaah-ALL the leetle ants are marching…*"

We pull around a corner and Josh heads over to an opening in the trees, where a bunch of vintage Gulfstream campers are parked all in a row. A group of people are hanging out, talking, setting up gear. Clearly, a party is starting. We get closer and people wave, shout greetings.

I'm speechless. They are beautiful, all of them, in the same carelessly rumpled way of Josh, Tommy, and Laurel. I feel like we're driving up to a catalog photo shoot, except there aren't any photographers or directors standing around, just a multicultural

dream of happy, shaggy, improbably pretty twen-
tysomethings.

Tommy parks. "This is it," he says. Josh hops
out and makes his way over toward a group of people setting up tables under a stand of trees.

Laurel turns to me. "Don't embarrass me," she
says. Her hair has somehow twisted and blown itself into a perfect corona around her perfect face.
Then she smiles. "I know you won't," she says.
"Just. Have fun."

A tall African-American guy with geek glasses
and a cowboy shirt strolls toward the car. He and
Tommy do that handshake hug thing and then he
gives Laurel a real hug. "And you are the little sister," he says.

"Brenda," I say.

"Brenda," he says. "Right. I'm Lee." I hold my
hand out for a shake and he laughs, pulls me in for
a hug. He smells like body spray and Mountain
Dew and something else. Food? Onions?

"So?" he says, pulling back. "You all ready?"

In the distance, I hear music start up. Drums.
Some kind of organ.

"Where are those guys?" Laurel says. "Did
they go all the way to Sunland? That's like the clos-
est one, right?"

Lee checks his phone. "Any minute now," he
says.

People are still bunched into little groups, mill-
ing around. I'm nervous and I pick at my cuticles,
stare at my feet. I look for a keg. Or a bar. I have
never been to this kind of party before, but I've

seen enough movies, watched enough television to know that somewhere, behind a car or a stand of trees, there's a keg sweating into a tub of ice. I scan the crowd. No red cups. No joints or cigarettes or anything. I remember what Laurel said before: "party supplies." I wonder if I'm ready for whatever this means.

Over behind the campers, a group of people are setting up what looks like a croquette court. "Are they…" I start.

Right then a car pulls in and Laurel whoops.

"Party's here," Lee says.

Four more guys get out of the car, each of them carrying two impossibly large McDonald's bags. They move purposefully toward the tables, nodding their heads at the shouts and claps from the rest of the group.

Laurel puts a hand on my shoulder. "It's happening," she says. She slips toward the tables. People are already eating hamburgers, high-fiving, bumping fists, nodding at one another with knowing looks in their eyes.

"Cheddar and ONION!" Josh shouts. He and Tommy bump fists.

The music stops and then starts again. "John Mayer about time!" Lee says. "Turn that shit up, y'all!"

I'm wondering if I'm being punked. Hamburgers? McDonald's? John Mayer and the Dave Matthews Band? This can't really be what Laurel's parties are like.

But then Laurel grabs a burger and takes a bite.

She closes her eyes and smiles and chews and she's beautiful and all of the sudden it's like that part of her that's secret, that she keeps just for her, is shining there in the late afternoon light, glowing, beckoning. I'm walking before I realize it. Then I'm running. As I get closer to the tables, I catch the first whiff of food—onion and cheese and a warm hint of grease—and I realize how hungry I've been all along.

DirecTV

Here is what I know. They wear tights. Their wings are thin flapping things that look more like they belong on dragonflies than butterflies. They never seem to get cold, don't shiver or shake or get soggy like the half a turkey sub they've been loitering next to for almost two weeks now. They don't eat: everything in the refrigerator is exactly the same as it was twelve days ago, which was exactly the same as it was thirteen days ago. Truth is everything is the same since Carrie left. Everything but the faeries.

All they talk about is football and the contents of the refrigerator and how I'm watching television, which the black one says is all wrong but that makes even less sense than the white one's jokes about Carrie's tapenade.

Even Carrie didn't have an opinion on how I watched television. Maybe if she comes back, they can have a roundtable, a panel discussion on my television failures and all the rest of it, too. They can invite her sister and her mother and her boss. They can talk about my emotional isolation and the Packers game, about the last time I said "I love you" and the right kind of things to be putting on a burger, about trial separations and low monthly fees.

I don't know whether to clean out the refrigerator or seal it up with duct tape and try to cut off their air supply. I don't know what would happen if I tried to grab them, stuff them into the garbage with the thongs and the hair supplies and the shampoos, the overdue Visa notices and the Good Housekeepings and the rest of the stuff Carrie left behind. I wonder what would happen if I zapped them with Raid. I wonder what would happen if Carrie came back, gave me a hug and said this was all a big misunderstanding, opened up the fridge to have herself some tapenade and a Miller Lite.

I wonder what would happen if I actually just bought Direct fucking TV like the black one keeps harping about.

I don't know why I haven't tried any of this yet. I don't know when I stopped talking to Carrie about my goddam day.

What I have tried is standing in the kitchen, smoking Parliament Lights and listening to the refrigerator. Every now and then, I take a quick peek to make sure they're still there. I slam the door as soon as the black one starts jabbering.

No matter how many times this happens, I'm always a little surprised when they're still in there. I put my ear up to the refrigerator. A low hum: gray machine noise and the chatter from the black one, the dull slap of a tiny football being passed back and forth. Chatter slap. Chatter slap. The white one makes a joke about the tapenade and I shout Goddamit and everything goes quiet except for the refrigerator hum.

I take a step back. I know what's coming. "How

you gonna watch the Redskins on Sunday?!?!" the black one shouts.

"Nothing like a little West Coast Offense and... tapenade," the white one deadpans.

I back into the living room, go to the window and peek through the crack in the curtains. It looks exactly the same out there, but how could that be?

In the few moments when I sleep, I can hear them talking and I'm not sure any more if it's in my head or really coming from the refrigerator. When I close my eyes, I see their little wings flapping.

I want to turn on the television but I wonder what the black one means about how I'm doing it wrong. I feel like I should be hungry but what kind of food would the white one think I should eat? I hate the way he says it—"tapenade"—with a sarcastic drip at the end, like what he's really saying is all those things Carrie said when she was stuffing her shit into the gym bag while her boss's Hummer whirred in the driveway.

Tapenade is pretty good. Olives and oil and capers, maybe some anchovies if that's what you're into. Carrie liked it. Likes it. What the hell is so funny about olives and capers and oil? I never hear the white one making jokes about salsa. He never says anything about hummus.

Fucking tapenade. It's not even mine, but I guess now it is.

I sneak into the kitchen and open the refrigerator door. "Hey man!" the black one says. "How you gonna watch gunslinging sensation Andrew Luck taking on his former coach, Jim Harbaugh?"

The white one just stands there, wings flapping. He looks goofier than usual. He sits down on an egg carton, doesn't even notice that his right wing is pushing up against the mustard. "I'm cold," he says.

"Come on, man," the black one whispers. He jerks his head in my direction. "Stand up, Peyton. What you think of that tapenade anyway?" He says the word like he's floating a softball, like the white one is gonna knock it out of the park.

But he just stands there, shakes his head. Every time his wings flap, a little halo of residue comes off them. "Too long," he says. "It's..." He puts his head in his hands. "Where are we, Prime?" he says.

I reach in and hold my hand up to him like I'm approaching a strange dog.

"Hey brother," the black one says, to me, "maybe you want to come back later. Give us a sec."

I put a finger up to the white one's wings. They are soft but crisp, something running through them like veins. I stroke the wing and he sighs. My eyes well up, white noise roars in my ears. My heart pounds and I wonder how many days it's been since she left. Fourteen? Two weeks? Can that be right? I wonder how many weeks before then since we actually sat down and talked about something more than the bills, the dishes, who was doing what to who on the *Real Housewives* or *Survivor*.

I hold out my hand and the white one stumbles into my palm. He's surprisingly heavy, solid. The wings stop flapping and go flaccid, the right one hanging down at a bad angle. He curls up into the fetal position. I move him over toward the counter, leave the door open so the other one can see. I put a trembling finger up to his wings and wonder if I can really feel the heartbeat in there or if I'm going crazy for good.

Taco Bell

A new email dings into his box and Miller cringes. Somehow he knows it's from her, something about the ding—it is insistent, urgent, as sure as a poke in the back of the neck. This will be message number 168 in this particular thread alone, the one with the subject line "The Steak."

The test kitchen is quiet, Green and Jefferson huddled in the corner, no doubt working through the Cool Ranch Burrito that HQ has made the group's second priority. It will never happen, Miller knows. He himself developed the Dorito taco shell, and that was difficult enough. A full wrap, a burrito wrap, no less, is as close to impossible as this particular area of food science gets.

The company's first priority, of course, is Chef Garcia, whose name stands bold in his Outlook: CHEF LORENA GARCIA. He knows it is no mistake that she has chosen to announce herself with capital letters. Perhaps she actually does have a custom ding has paid some entity somewhere to ensure the auditory prominence of her messages over their electronic rivals.

At this point, he would believe anything.

CHEF LORENA GARCIA. The email might as well be ticking.

He can hear her voice: "Guys! We have to do better, guys." That clear enunciation, flat and insistent. The light accent. The humorless certainty of celebrity. More than once over the past several months, he has heard that voice honking at the edges of his mind. In a crowded coffee shop, at the mall, walking down the street, in the background noise of a televised sporting event. "GUYS."

Green and Jefferson are bent over, peeking through the window of the test oven. Not a good sign.

CHEF LORENA GARCIA. He waves his cursor over the name.

Twenty-five years at Yum! Brands and Miller has never come across anybody with this combination of blind confidence, lack of understanding of the limitations of the production environment, pure commitment, and agency. She is a perfect storm.

More than once over these past several months, he has fantasized about what it would be like to be dominated sexually by Chef Lorena Garcia. This is an idea that had never entered his head before. But lately, like that voice, these images, these sensations—desires?—have slipped into his consciousness, and they return with greater frequency the longer this project lasts. He can't help but imagine the scene: himself on all fours, Chef Lorena Garcia standing over him, pushing at his buttock with the point of a heel. "Guys!" she would say. "We have to do better guys." And she would poke the heel deeper into his flesh, rotating slowly.

He slumps in his chair, clicks on "CHEF LORE-NA GARCIA" quick and hard, like he is eliminating an electronic pest in some kind of video game.

He sees the first word—"GUYS"—and hops out of his chair.

He walks toward the windows. It is getting dark and he watches traffic moving haltingly on the interstate. The most amazing thing, he thinks, is how much she cares. It is remarkable, monstrous. The thread called "The Avocado" reached so many emails that they had to create a new one called "The Avocado Too." The "too" was his own touch, an attempt at levity that was lost on Chef Lorena Garcia, and so the first 17 emails in that thread are given over to grammar lessons and recriminations and a discussion of what is funny and where it is appropriate.

He has pictured all kinds of scenarios. What she would be like in bed, on a commuter bus, at a dinner party. He imagines her as a workmanlike conversationalist, the kind of person who has taken a class in small talk: how to break the ice, steer the conversation, look people in the eye and gently mimic their body language.

The voice comes into his head again. "GUYS! Lose the burrito and share these beautiful ingredients with the world."

Miller thinks of the thousand reasons this cannot be done. He wonders what Lorena Garcia pictures when she thinks of him, the person to whom she has sent these 168 emails, each of them featuring some version of the kinds of demands one would give to a sous chef.

"GUYS! Lose the tortilla and share these beautiful ingredients with the world."

Miller looks at the computer, at the bathroom exit sign, at all the papers on his desk. They are Taco Bell. Lose the tortilla?

He is certain that she does not drive her own vehicle, that she would never exercise in a public place, that each time she appears on television, another layer of her Venezuelan accent has been diligently scrubbed.

Her last email simply said:

"If you want to show people you're changing, show them you're changing."

He wonders what this could possibly mean. It could be a zen koan. It could be something Lorena Garcia read in a self-help book or overheard on *SportsCenter*.

Surely they should have told her. This not cooking. This isn't *Top Chef*. This is food science: test environment, marketing, user testing, research, packaging, the extreme limitations of making food that can be reproduced at any Taco Bell in any country in any part of the world. It was near impossible to roll out grilled chicken, and now this woman is sending email instructions like "share these beautiful ingredients with the world."

These ingredients are not beautiful. They are workmanlike, mass produced. This is why there are 168 emails about The Steak.

He has paged through the Victoria's Secret catalogs that still come addressed to Clair. He imagines that Lorena Garcia would wear the kind of panties they used to call "boyshorts" until recently, when they took on the name "cheekies." She would buy them from Macy's, or whatever store sells the most expensive cheekies. She would send a female assistant with specific instructions about colors and sizes and the importance of never revealing the name of the person who would be wearing these cheekies beneath her chef's whites.

Where did this person even come from, he wonders. She was a guest on *Top Chef* and the next thing he knows she is bossing him around from airports and hotel lobbies all over the world. He knows that as soon as he's through this, they'll foist that lantern-jawed Aussie Curtis Stone on him. Somebody at one of the companies that owns the others now is convinced that Curtis Stone is the next Rachel Ray, and Miller can see the day that Chef Curtis Stone is sending him emails that begin: "MATES."

He shivers in his chair.

Green and Jefferson are pulling things out of the test oven and Miller can tell by their reactions that the results are not positive. Something in him relaxes. If they are able to pull the Dorito burrito off, his own failures with Chef Garcia will seem even worse.

Green throws a burrito at the garbage can and misses. It leaves a familiar reddish-brown Rorschach on the floor. Everybody in this kitchen has seen that color dripping off a wall, has scraped it off shoes and shirts, memos and keyboards and computer screens.

Chef Lorena Garcia has a similar coloring, her natural Venezuelan skin augmented, Miller imagines, with some kind of high-end tanning solution available exclusively to the rich and famous. He wonders if she has tan lines. He imagines she does not.

He wonders if she is like this in other areas of her life. Is she this immovable, this sure all the time? Or is this just with food? What is life like for her agent, the person who books her travel, her realtor and her assistant?

This has been his life for the past several months, what his married colleagues refer to as a "honey do" list.

He's not sure why, but he is positive that, like him, Lorena Garcia has no family. He has never even considered her as a mother, a spouse. After these past few years, he can recognize another person who is alone.

He stares at the screen, that blinking cursor, the bold name CHEF LORENA GARCIA.

Green and Jefferson are packing up for the day.

He sits back in his chair.

CHEF LORENA GARCIA.

Brown and Jefferson shuffle out of the office. They are carrying no test subjects with them.

DING!

An email pops into his box. "The Avacado Too" number 216.

DING! "The Steak" number 169.

DING! "LOSE THE TORTILLA!"

Miller shifts in his chair. He looks to the exits. What the hell could she be doing?

One more email dings into the box and he turns.

He looks at the ground. It is dirty. He wonders when they stopped vacuuming the floors in the offices. Sometime around the mid-2000s, when they stopped replacing the trash can liners. He is lucky to have this job.

Outside, it is dark. "If you want to show people you're changing, show them you're changing." He thinks he knows what this means. He wonders if he is right.

He turns back to his email. CHEF LORENA GARCIA. In the subject line, she's written three words, small caps: "ARE YOU OKAY?"

Lexus

Cynthia wakes to coffee smell and the sounds of William getting breakfast ready for the kids. She closes her eyes and for a moment, it is as if everything is normal. Like last Christmas, the one before, like every holiday since they made the move from Hoboken to Greenwich. She holds onto the idea of normal, pushes away the questions, the dark thoughts that wait like traps at the edges of her mind, and lets the sensations take over: the twelve-hundred thread count Kate Spade sheets, the smell of cinnamon buns and coffee, the Christmas music, the kids shouting and asking when they can start unwrapping presents. For a few glowing moments, it is as if all the pieces of her wonderful life are still anchored in place.

But then the glow deadens again and what's left is the pit in her stomach, the pressure on her bowels, the feeling like she's caught in an undertow, being sucked toward some blank horizon.

She rushes to the bathroom and releases her bowels. Nerves, the doctor said. The stress of the holidays. If only he knew. The wine is still heavy in her head, and she wonders how many bottles they drank last night, how much of their ghostly portfolio is currently emptying into the toilet. She remembers the fire, the television's white babble, each of them playing with their iPads. Pouring more wine.

She remembers William hinting at a present, making puns that she didn't quite understand. She remembers that last night was one more night he didn't tell her. At the time, she was furious, but now, sitting on the toilet with the sounds of Christmas—normal, wonderful Christmas—happening just downstairs, she doesn't know whether to ascribe his continuing silence to hubris or chivalry.

She runs some water on her face, avoids the mirror, and stumbles into the walk-in closet. She wobbles, steadies herself on a Dolce & Gabbana she had bought for last year's holiday party. What was the excuse William had made for no party this year? Redecorating the office. She wonders if the rest of the partners are in the same situation or if they've been wiser, more careful, at least, with their personal finances.

Christmas music tinkles up through the foyer. John Denver and the Muppets. This is William's favorite, and in typical fashion, he has tried every year to get her and then the twins interested. She estimates they have had this album in three different forms: cassette, CD, and now, finally, streaming from whatever new service William is favoring at the moment. He has always been like this: relentless, resilient, unwilling or unable to take no for an answer. She has known for years that, eventually, the twins would give in and realize that they love Muppet Christmas almost much as their dad, the same way she gave in more than twenty years ago, the same way various department heads and vice presidents had made way as he willed himself toward the upper reaches of Canaan Capital.

"Cynthia," he calls. "We're ready down here." There's something in his voice, pride swelling. Anticipation. She is torn between not wanting to know anything, and wanting to know every single thing.

She puts on a Pucci wrap and her Ugg slippers. She wonders if they'll be able to keep the clothes. Are the clothes paid for? She realizes it's been years since she's seen a Visa bill.

She walks to the hall, shouts "coming!" down toward the kitchen. After so many years in the two-bedroom in Hoboken, it took them some time to get used to these nearly six thousand square feet. At first, it was just the two of them. Then the dogs, and then, after two years of trying normally and five frustrating IVF cycles, the twins. Now the place seems the perfect size. Each of them has a room, each of the adults an office. The au pair has her suite. The children have their playroom. The dogs, their basement. The gardeners, their lawn.

She wonders how long it would take to clean the house by herself. She realizes she's never even tried. She looks at the walk-in closet, as large as their entire Hoboken apartment. Her friends tend to romanticize those early days of struggle, of two mid-level incomes, but she knows that this is what they always wanted. Both of them. When they did leave Hoboken it was with the Springsteen surety of small town college graduates making out for the big city. They were destined for Greenwich, for this, and so this is where they wound up.

"Mom!" Clarice shouts. "We want to open our

presents!"

She sits down on the comforter. Part of her wishes she didn't know a thing. She was looking for an Evite invitation, of all things. He was in the shower and she needed directions. His phone was on. She opened his email and saw the subject line "Options without bankruptcy" and the name of their accountant.

She has made her peace with losing the house, but it is all the rest of it that she's dreading: the pity in her sister's voice, the questions from the kids, the fact that William has carried on for these past months like nothing has changed, has kept up appearances, plowed ahead with his usual dogged good humor as if the only concern is whether to vacation in Bali or Saint Lucia.

She makes her way downstairs, staring at her feet as she goes. When she gets to the bottom, she sees them lined up, William and the twins, at the door.

"What?" she says.

"Let's take a look outside," William says. "Looks like Santa thought somebody was awfully good this year."

The rumble returns to her belly. What could he possibly be doing? What is he thinking? She shoots him a look, but he is too busy high-fiving Samuel and then Clarice to notice.

"It's pretty awesome, Mom," Samuel says. The boy smiles William's smile—confident, carefree. She wonders what public school would do to that smile.

William swings open the door and the first thing she sees, framed in the entryway, is a giant red ribbon. She walks outside in a daze. William steps aside to reveal a silver SUV. A Lexus. The out-size ribbon makes the car look like a giant match-box. Her first instinct is to turn back to the house. Her second, to start driving and not stop. It is cold outside and she pulls the shawl tight on her shoulders. She sees the O'Connells walking by with their twin corgis and wonders what they could possibly think of this display.

"William…" she starts. And then she sees it. He is tapping his foot, pulling at the cuticle of his right thumb. French. She thinks. French 202. Junior year at Brown. His mind, so efficient and calculating in finance or math, couldn't comprehend the intricacies of verb conjugation, couldn't make the transition from utilitarian English to the fluid music of French. They would sit down to study and he would start up right away, picking at the cuticles like they held an answer, tapping his feet nervously. He would emerge from tests bloody-thumbed and silent.

"What do you think?" he says, trying for the usual smile. He picks at one thumb, then the other. The children are already in the car, wondering at the smell, the mounted DVDs in the back seat, the USB ports and dashboard like a spaceship from some movie. Something in his face changes and she realizes that he knows. He knows she knows, has all along.

She holds her hands out and he throws her the

keys. "It's wonderful," she says.

Viagra

The real cowboy wears a fishing cap and one of those vests you associate with photographers, only his isn't stuffed with film or lenses or malaria pills so much as his cigarettes and a lighter, breath spray, and three burner cell phones. He has mean, intelligent, too-close eyes, and hair the color of Darkest Brown Just for Men Shampoo-in Hair Coloring. I know about the hair because he tells me about it every morning. First thing he does when we get to the shoot is shake my hand, giggle at my salt-and-pepper, then make a big show about running a hand through his greasy, mocha hair and wondering out loud how these "Madison Avenue pussies" could hire a schoolteacher to play a cowboy and a cowboy to teach the schoolteacher.

The real cowboy sidles over now and does the whole routine. He waits for me to react. I know it's some kind of challenge and I know I've been failing it every day, three days running now.

"Well..." I say. I never know what to say to him, and the prospect of not having to talk to him, ever again, is the only thing I'm looking forward to when we end the shoot this afternoon.

"Well what?" he says, taking a step in my direction. He's short and I can see the dandruff in his Darkest Brown Just for Men. "Well what?" he says again. He's not one of those people who will let you make an indefinite statement and then drift off. He would be hell in one of those awkward new sitcoms.

"You think you can show me that thing with the rope again?" I say. What I've realized is it doesn't really matter what I ask him. Something about the shoot—the rope I'm supposed to swing around, the saddle I lift up toward the camera, how a cowboy would sit on a horse—he'll demonstrate quickly, get it out of the way, then start talking about something else, hitting one of his talking points. He likes to tell stories about victories over retail clerks: the time he bullied himself into a free dinner at Applebee's, when he got the middle eastern cashier at Home Depot fired, what he said when he thought the gay guy at the feed mill had shortchanged him.

He likes to talk about what he would do to Cindy, who plays the woman my character is probably taking a pill to have sex with.

They found us both in bars, me and the real cowboy, although not the same one. His was a roadhouse the advance people had tiptoed into to find "for-real fucking cowboys." Mine was a P. F. Chang's in the mall where I was waiting tables at night. They stopped in for a bite. I asked if they wanted some dynamite shrimp. They looked at each other and handed me a card.

"Okay everybody! We're wrapping up in the office. Next scene is the cowboy," the AD shouts. This is the one I've been waiting for: me and Cindy goofing around with a lasso.

"Here's your big one!" the real cowboy says.

He pokes me in the ribs and it hurts. One of his phones buzzes and he looks at the number. "Stupid bitch," he says and stuffs it back in the vest.

We're standing by the craft table. I pick at the roast beef and I wonder about my breath, but then I remember we're not really going to be having sex, or kissing, or anything, really—just looking like people who definitely might want to have sex in one to four hours.

Cindy comes over and fills up a bowl of granola, adds some almond milk. She nods at both of us and wanders over toward her trailer. We both watch her go.

"What I wouldn't do to that," the real cowboy says. "Or is it, what I *didn't* do?" He reaches into a pocket on his vest, pulls out a handful of little blue pills. He pops two into his mouth, puts two next to the roast beef on my plate.

"What are you doing?" I say.

"They don't mind."

"Where did you get those?"

"For your big scene," he says.

"Where did you get those?" I ask again.

"Where would you not? Look the fuck around." He waves a hand toward the rented farm, the silos and the highway stretching off in the distance, the trailers that line the driveway. "You go into one of those trailers," he says, "there are boxes of the things. Boxes."

"I don't want to take that," I say.

"People pay good money for these things," he says. "Not that I need it. Thought, you know," he takes off his hat and runs a hand through his hair, "you might could use it."

"We're going to be standing in a field," I say. "Messing around with a lasso."

"He thinks he's gonna be the first man lassoing with a hard-on," he says. His phone buzzes again and he hits reject.

"It could take an hour. You know how slow this is. These cameras. All these people standing around."

"She has her own trailer," he says. I pretend to be checking my phone. He turns to our left, to an imaginary person. "And he says he's not married. Or gay neither." He pauses. "Oh I know. I know!" he retorts, laughing at a joke I can't hear. "But that's what he says."

"This is ridiculous," I say.

He turns back to me. "She's worth it," he says, pokes me again, right in the belly. "Believe me."

"That's just crazy," I say. "This is crazy."

"Who you think's been calling me?" He holds out the phone then shuts it before I can see what it says on the little screen. He takes a step toward me. His boot is resting only an inch from my shoe. I can see his molars, gray and shallow, when he talks. "I thought you seemed like a pussy," he says. "Takes a real man to do a real man's job. Fake man to stand in a field, play around with a real man's rope."

I take a step back, put some distance between us. I think about the empty apartment and the school year starting up again soon, what I'm going to hear from my middle school students if this commercial ever airs. I look at the pills: light blue and tiny. They look like candy, like Smarties or Skittles.

"Just because I'm not a real cowboy..." I start, but I don't know how to finish.

"We'll see," he says. He jabs at me like he's going to throw a punch, pulls back and laughs. He walks slow, toward the trailer, and shakes his head. I turn the pills over in my hand.

Coors Light

It is noon. Very hot. The Denver sun's pitiless spotlight pushes down upon pedestrians carrying briefcases or carryout lunches. Like ants under a child's magnifying glass, they skitter along the baking sidewalks, retreat under awnings, scurry back into the comfort of their air conditioned holes. I take my place on the bench. As always, I watch.

Today is the day. I am sure of it. Today is the reason I am here. The answer. Today is why I found myself driving west last month with no more plan or control than a monarch flapping toward Mexico.

The crowd moves along, north and south and east and west. They think today is like any other day but I can tell it is different. There is something about the sun today. Something about Him today.

He stops on the crowded sidewalk. Do it, I think. Whatever it is. Do it.

He is young. Mid-twenties. Casually handsome. Dressed like he's going a nightclub. Too dressed for this heat. He stops, looks to the sky.

I stand, take a few hesitant steps toward Him. I am not the only one to notice. Nearby, pedestrians give way, pause, watch as he wipes his brow, shakes his head, reaches a tentative hand to the sky.

Of course, I think. Of course! I laugh and the woman standing next to me shoots me a glance. Don't you see? I want to ask her. Of course it was there all along.

He continues reaching. How is it possible? That can't be, I think, even as the arm elongates and advances, reaching and reaching... for what? The crowd gasps. It can't be, but then it is: he palms the sun. The sky goes dark.

Half of the bystanders run. "Nine-eleven!" somebody shouts, and more people scurry.

This can't be happening but the sky has gone dark and he is holding the sun and it is happening and now I'm laughing full out because of course this is happening. Of course this is why I am here. This is why I awoke that day in Philadelphia and drove without stopping for so much as a microwave burrito until I reached this intersection. This can't be happening but I knew the first time I saw Him that He was the one for whom I had been delivered. My car was towed long ago and I haven't slept in weeks but now it is happening and I thank whatever god has allowed me to be here. I thank Him.

Cars stop. Traffic lights go dark. There is a rumble and a crash and what feels like a tremor in the earth. "The subway!" somebody shouts. More people scurry but even more move even closer toward Him.

I am confident now and I pick my way through the bystanders, past muttering businessmen and teenagers saying the rosary, past a group of cub scouts who are gathered together in prayer, a man and woman kissing passionately. They don't understand that this is only the beginning. Somehow,

I do.

He looks about the darkened cityscape. He turns to the left, where a line of immobilized traffic trickles out of a tunnel. I have been living in this intersection for weeks and have come to regard this tunnel as a hazard, a place to be avoided, a source of constant noise and certain danger. I know the police walk this tunnel, two of them and a dog, at dawn and again at dusk.

He regards the orb glowing in his hand, the only source of light in the suddenly quiet city. Do it, I think. Or do I say it out loud? It is impossible to tell now. He takes a step and hurls the sun into the darkest black of the tunnel. Suddenly, light. Sound. Music?

I notice that I am no longer hot. It is as if the earth's air conditioner has been turned on, like the cool edge of a hurricane.

In the distance, a low rumble. A train?

We turn to look en masse and a gleaming silver locomotive explodes out of the tunnel.

I want to drop to my knees, to praise him, ask for forgiveness, but I'm buoyed by the music: *People all over the world...*

I want to go to Him, to pledge my devotion, to ask what does it mean, what is next, but there is already a long line of women writing phone numbers on little scraps of paper.

The train thunders past and I'm surprised but then—of course!—not surprised at all to find something cool and wet in my hand. I bring the glistening container to my mouth and drink deeply—water, a faint taste of hops and tin. It is delicious. It tastes… is it possible to taste *cold?* Of course anything is possible and this is the coldest tasting drink I've ever had and look at him dancing and taking phone numbers and I know that this is so much better than the first time, the water into wine and no mention of trains or dancing or miniskirts or the sweet nickel spark of *cold* on your taste buds, and then I take another drink and join the crowd and we dance and the locomotive thunders and we sing into the noisy chasm: *like a Love Train, Love Train.*

Intuit GoPayment

Derek barely slows down at intersections. Not anymore. Not since we got that card reader and "set out toward the sun."

Right now, we're somewhere in Virginia or North Carolina, barreling eighty miles an hour down 77 south. It's been twenty hours since we left Columbus and we've only stopped twice—once for gas, and once when I told him I'd pee right in the truck if he didn't pull over.

I can see the intersection up ahead, green interstate signs forming an entryway, a decision-point: we need to head west on 81 or stay on 77. He glances at me and I look down, act like I'm paying attention to the little blue dot moving along the map on my phone, like I'm tracking it, planning, like there's some kind of logic happening in our movements. Like we're not driving an ice cream truck twenty-five miles over the speed limit with no direction other than Derek's wheel-jerking intuition.

He gives me the look, the one he wants to say "isn't this awesome?" What it really says is, "this has to be awesome. If this isn't awesome, then…"

A text pops on my phone, Lupe again: "Are we opening? WHERE R YOU GUYS?" I picture her standing outside the shop with James and Tina, the college kids we hired this summer. First thing we should have done when everything started slow-ing down was let them go, settle up with Lupe, tell her there'd be an Assistant Manager job waiting in the Spring. There are lots of things we should have done.

The road signs are almost overhead. Derek laughs and spins the wheel to the right and the truck lurches, careens under the 77 south sign. We nearly collide with a UPS truck and all I can hear is the horn blasting, the sound so loud that even though I'm only two feet away from him, I can't even hear Derek shouting "toward the sun!"

•

We bought the store soon after the doctor said we couldn't get pregnant. We looked at the alternatives—in vitro, international adoption—the cost was almost the same. "Transference" is what the marriage counselor called it, with a question in her voice and eyes looking right at me. Derek just shook his head, took my hand, said thanks but no thanks and we better not be charged for this session.

"We met in a fucking Baskin Robbins," he said, while we were walking out the door.

I gave the counselor a look like Sorry, and she nodded her head in a way I knew meant Good Luck.

•

I wake up to the stop-go left-right of the truck moving through a neighborhood. For a groggy moment I think we're back in Columbus, driving through Clintonville or the University District. It's a nice thought—we had some good days this summer, days that made it seem like everything was going to be okay.

But then I sit up, check the phone. It is three AM and I have twelve text messages. Large McMansions roll by on all sides—glass and brick, two car garages, spotlights on landscaped yards.

"What are we doing?" I say. I look at the map on my phone. "We're in Raleigh?"

The truck smells like ice cream and Fritos and sweat. My neck is cramping and my knees are sore. "I need to get out of this truck for a while," I say.

"Soon," he says. He slows down, looks from house to house.

"Do you know somebody here?" I ask.

He keeps on driving. On the right, a completely dark house. He cuts the engine and we coast to a stop. Derek gives me the Look, taps me on the leg, then runs around to the back of the house. I sit in the truck and wait, tell myself he must be going to the bathroom. Something. I check my first text. My mother: "Where are you we are getting worried."

I lean back, close my eyes. How could I even begin to explain?

I'm not sure how long I'm asleep before the door opens and Derek comes in. He throws a gym bag in the back seat and starts the engine. "What was that?" I ask.

"Toward the sun," he says.

•

The first few months of the shop, everything was great. We hired Lupe and the college kids. We were making money, working together every day. We were too busy to think about that word—transference—and the look on the marriage counselor's face.

Then right after graduation, everything started to go sour. It was a bad September: cold and rainy in Columbus. There were days when we had more employees in the store than customers, weeks when we lost hundreds of dollars.

We were right in the middle of researching bankruptcy when Derek started whispering "toward the sun" to me at odd times—in the middle of the night, when he was heading out to pick up the paper, in the middle of washing the dishes. "Toward the sun," he would say, and he'd wink, get that look on his face. "Toward. The. Sun."

•

We stop at a truck stop.

"It's getting warmer!" he says.

I look at my phone. Twenty-four text messages. I don't think I can even read them. I wonder if my mother has sent the police to the house, when Lupe and the kids finally decided we weren't opening and went home.

Derek is right, though: it is getting warmer. According to my phone, we're near Savannah, and the warm air feels like it's hugging me, like all that's keeping me from floating away are the shoes on my feet.

"Maybe this wasn't such a bad idea," I say.

"Who said it was a bad idea?" Derek says. His hair has gone crazy. He needs to shave and I can smell him through the gas fumes.

"Nothing," I say.

•

It wasn't so much that we couldn't get pregnant as we didn't know what to do next. That was the logical thing on the list, the next step. Right up until then, everything was going according to schedule: full time jobs, 401k, three bedrooms and two baths on three-quarters of an acre.

We were careful people, methodical, and everything was working. And then, all of the sudden, it was like the plan itself had betrayed us. We came home, sat down on the couch, turned on the TV, and looked at each other.

•

Derek follows signs to Myrtle Beach and before I know it we're at the ocean. We stumble out of the truck and look at the waves. It is beautiful. Warm. Ice cream weather.

Derek turns on the outside speaker, flips the converter for the chest freezer, opens up a box of sugar cones and a box of regular, jacks the GoPayment thing into his phone. He turns on the music. I stand behind him.

There's not a soul on the beach.

"What's going on?" he says.

I check my phone. "It's Thanksgiving," I say.

He nods, turns the music up, and "Mister Softee" blares out over the empty beach. I look to the ocean, the place where the waves turn from choppy to smooth. I know we'll stay here, knuckles gripping the welcome window like the sides of a life raft, until the sun goes down and the ice cream weather turns chilly, and it's finally time to go home.

KFC

You are not the kind of guy who would be at a place like this at this time in the evening. But here you are, and you cannot say the terrain is entirely unfamiliar. You are at a party, talking to a girl. A pretty girl with sleepy eyes and messy hair and jeans that you suspect came from WalMart. She is wearing Uggs. You are drinking a Natural Light and becoming increasingly self-conscious about your Western shirt and clean shave and the baggie of Bolivian Marching Powder that sits in your front pocket like a detonator.

How did you get here? It was your new friend, Ted Reichenbach, who powered you in here, and he has disappeared. You started the evening with margaritas at Outback and then moved on to shots and beer at Applebee's before a round of Ultimate Long Island Iced Teas at TGI Fridays. Ted prefers the constant motion of bar tours, the familiar safety of national chain restaurants. Ted says things like "pre-game" and "get our drink on." Ted calls you "bro."

You met Ted in the mailroom of your new condo. He was friendly and you were tired of watching Netflix by yourself. The few times you had gone out alone were a disaster—nights spent hitting refresh on Twitter while your DC friends posted updates from clubs you had never heard of, bars that had sprouted up since your departure.

Now Ted is gone, having followed a girl in a hippie dress through the patio doors and out toward the cornfield that adjoins the back yard of this one-story ranch house. You are not used to these kinds of parties—in somebody's house, classic rock blaring from the kitchen, people watching television or playing quarters. Not anymore. Not for, how long has it been since high school? Six, seven years.

The girl in the Uggs is talking about Penn State football in the earnest tones that your DC friends reserved for punk pioneers, dead male writers, or certain politicians. Her eyes are bright blue, with halos of brown around the edges. She says something about a linebacker and you nod and sneak a peek down her shirt.

You look around. The house is run-down, with orange shag carpeting and thrift shop landscapes on the walls. A bucket of KFC sits on a table next to a jar of supermarket salsa. In the living room, a group of guys are watching Super Troopers, drinking purposefully from green bottles.

You wonder about the Bolivian Marching Powder. Would the girl be cool with it? It's hard to tell with people around here. It's been three months since you were transferred and you still can't exactly peg them. You finish your beer and grab another. You have no idea what this girl is talking about, and everything is starting to feel fuzzy and quick.

The girl excuses herself, touches your chest and says she really wants to hang out but right now she has to go tell Renee that she's an asshole and a slut. You nod, look to see if she is joking, but she makes no indication either way.

You check your phone. It is ten o' clock. If you were still in DC, you'd be taking shots at West's apartment on Fourteenth Street, texting and tweeting about where you might start out, where you might end up, what might happen in between. You'd be laying out lines of Bolivian Marching Powder.

You finish your beer and look for the girl in the Uggs. She is in the living room, hugging another girl—pudgy, wearing a flannel shirt and the same knockoff jeans. Somebody has changed the music, and an old Eminem song blares through the house. The Super Trooper guys stand in a loose circle, making a shambles of the lyrics, their fingers twisted into mock gang signs. They have moved the KFC into the living room and you wonder if this is some kind of racist joke, but then you notice that two of them are waving drumsticks around like microphones, and write it off to the munchies.

Which brings you back to the Bolivian Marching Powder. You slip into the bathroom, cut a few lines. The rush hits you immediately. Your first thought: this is the last of it. After tonight, you'll have to go back to DC for more. Your second thought: this is the worst party you've been to in your entire life. You check your nose in the mirror, pop the baggie in your pocket, and walk out the door.

Ted is waiting. "Hey man," he says. "This is

lame. Let's roll. Next stop."

You look for the girl in the Uggs but she has vanished.

"Let's roll, bro," Ted says. He jingles his keys. "I know a place."

You wind through cornfields and along country roads. Ted sings along with an old Rush song on the radio. It is all classic rock here. You have heard more Billy Squier in the past three months than the entire 26 years prior. Ted lights a cigarette and rolls his window down. He pulls onto a main thoroughfare and you recognize where you are for the first time. The mall rolls by on the right. You pass a row of car dealerships, a factory, a Target. "There we go," Ted says.

"What?" you say.

He pulls into KFC and hops out of the car. You follow, still not sure if he's making a joke or not. It is too bright in here, hot under the fluorescent lights. The kids behind the counter move like hostages, thunking chicken into buckets with a scarcely concealed disgust. Ted orders a bucket and you follow him to a booth.

"Here we go," he says. "Party time." He smiles and pushes the bucket in your direction.

You finger the baggie in your pocket. You check your phone. No messages.

Toyota

Burns looks out toward the road. He puts a hand up to the glass and shakes his head. "I can't believe this," he says, his breath fogging the double-paned, oversized bay windows. "You're not going to believe this!" he shouts. In the background, the static babble of the *Real Housewives*, shouting and laughing and chairs scraping. "Rachel!" he says. Nothing. He can see the back of her head, framed by the television in the living room. He wonders if she's awake, if she even hears him anymore, if her ears have evolved into a plane where his frequency no longer registers among the screeches and threats of the glass-clinking, drink-throwing Housewives.

He turns back to the window, watches the Best Buy delivery guys struggle to carry his neighbor's new flatscreen up the winding walk. They make jokes and shake their heads, stop to adjust their grips. The thing is gigantic. Sixty-five inches at least. Maybe seventy-five. Eighty? He wonders how large they get. It is as if they are lugging a grand piano up to Nichols' place.

Burns turns around and looks at his own forty-six inch Samsung, glimmering in the living room. It is tiny, a joke. His wife's head is no longer visible and he wonders whether she has retreated to the bedroom or if she's playing possum on the couch. On the television, a row of women are lined up, all of them shouting at once. A smirking host taps no-tecards on his knees, mugs for the camera.

The workmen stand by the doorway. Nichols comes out with bottles of water for everybody. They make jokes, their hands held down as if carrying the television, scaled wide in reference to its sheer size. It's a party over there. A giant television party.

Burns remembers standing in that same Best Buy not so much as five weeks ago. A salesman had quietly pulled him aside, assured him that he didn't want to get bigger than fifty, that the size was there but the technology wasn't ready. Burns had been skeptical of the guy from the start: a salesman with dreadlocks and a neck tattoo? Burns remembers when salesmen wore short sleeved shirts and black ties, pocket protectors and glasses, when they sold things that lasted for decades without service plans or replacement insurance.

But why would the guy lie? What could possibly be in it for him? Now Burns considers whether, somehow, Nichols could have been behind the whole thing.

The Best Buy guys lean the massive television box against the entry columns. Nichols walks them over to the driveway, where they regard his truck. He presses a button on his keychain and the one who seems to be in charge, a tall guy who looks like a football coach in a movie, nods approvingly. They high five.

Burns wanders back to the living room. There is no sign of Rachel, other than the lingering Housewives, now in swimsuits, drinking wine around some exotic pool. The picture is laser sharp, that much is true. But the television is, what, half the size of the one outside the Nichols place. Maybe two-thirds at best?

Burns returns to the window. The television box is unmarked and he wonders if it was some kind of special order. That would be just like Nichols. Just like the granite in the kitchen and bamboo floors and the laptops and the wireless surround sound in every room of the house. Just like the pool and the hot tub and the cabana. Just like the god-damn boat.

The boat.

Burns wants a drink. It is three o'clock on Saturday afternoon. Possibly too early for a drink, possibly not. "Rachel!" he shouts. He hears the toilet upstairs.

The boat was the worst of all. Burns bought the boat—a used, twenty-six-foot Bowrider, on a Saturday. They took it out on a Sunday. By Thursday of that week, Nichols was towing a forty-six-foot Sea Ray, brand new, up the driveway.

"Gotta say, neighbor," he had said. "You gave me the idea all right. No sense living this close to the bay without a boat, am I right?"

That was the last they had talked until they bumped into one another at Best Buy last week, Burns whispering in a corner with the dreadlocked salesman, Nichols leading a pack of sales people around the Apple section.

Burns pours himself two fingers of Templeton

Rye, nearly chokes on the whiskey burn. He wills himself to like it—the mixture of sweet and smoky. He has been a beer drinker all his life, but he can see why people like whiskey. It is distinctive, efficient, expensive. This Templeton isn't even sold in Maryland—had to be special ordered through some website he saw advertised in *Esquire*. He pours another two fingers, holds his breath and knocks it back.

He goes back to the window. The Best Buy guys are standing in the bed of Nichols' Toyota. He is, Burns knows, explaining something about the lining. Next he will demonstrate the Bluetooth. Then he'll bring them over to look at the boat.

Fuck it, Burns thinks. Then he says it out loud: "fuck it." He goes downstairs to the lockbox, finds the title, and grabs his keys. The sound of two Housewives shouting echoes through the house as he walks through the door.

•

All the sales people are busy—apparently, there's some kind of deal going on—so Burns marches up to the front desk and places his title on the counter. "May I help you?" a young woman asks.

Burns taps on the title, points toward the largest truck in the showroom. "Looking for a truck," he says. "Something that can pull my boat."

The woman nods her head. Burns knows he needs to be assertive, can't show any weakness with car dealerships. A sign in the corner says "No

Money Down and No Payments for 12 Months!"

The woman taps something into her computer. Burns flashes on Nichols driving that Sea Ray up the driveway, the way he said "neighbor."

"Well, our Tundra pulled the Space Shuttle," the woman says, a winking tone in her voice. "How big is your boat?"

Canada Dry

Excerpt from "Centers for Disease Control: Obesity in Central Florida," February 2019.

Wes Urban, 32 years of age, 298 lbs.

We weren't always like this. How fat we are is what I mean. Most of us, when we first came here, we looked like models, like extras in a beer commercial or one of them romantic comedies. Carrie Newgent? She was here on First Day, same as me. Lives over there at mile post 0.27, near the row of the green portajohns and the FEMA showers? She was one of the first in line. This is before we even knew why we were here, before anybody even asked why a little girl would set up a Ginger Ale stand in the middle of nowhere. I'm talking before the news and the government and what the people from Canada Dry did. Point is, what I'm saying, Carrie Newgent on First Day was a sight to see. Now she's I don't know how much. Big lady. Like everybody from First Day, everybody from Year One, Two, and on like that. Now, we're all big like this. Back then, though, man you should have seen us.

•

Excerpt from unreleased documentary, "The Canada Dry Girl," Central Florida, 2013.

Carrie Newgent, 29 years of age, 248 lbs.

Interviewer: What do you say to people who worry that the... drink... you're drinking. The ginger ale. Might have... addictive properties?

Carrie Newgent: [Laughs] It's ginger ale! Soda. Same as they drink everywhere in the world. Same as you get at the supermarket or the 7-11 or a baseball game. Here [holds out a soda], give it a shot.

Interviewer: I don't...

CN: It's soda pop!

Interviewer: Some people say the field... that there are qualities.

CN: The field? [Gestures behind her] It's dirt and ginger. You can see that for yourself. You can go over there stick your thumb in it if you like. Plenty have done it.

Interviewer: But this is the only place in the world where those two things—ginger and dirt is what I mean. Where they combine to produce manufactured ginger ale. In plastic bottles. Bottles that have been confirmed to contain no organic materials.

CN: Well. Are we talking about, I mean, are you asking about the soda or the field or us or the girl?

Interviewer: I'm asking about all of it, I suppose.

CN: Well. [Finishes can of ginger ale]. Maybe what you want to be asking about, then, is the girl.

•

Excerpt, Snopes.com:

Canada Dry Ginger Ale Girl. Central Florida. Aka, "The Girl."

Claim: That in a field in Central Florida, a girl, known as "The Ginger Girl," or by followers simply as "The Girl," is able to produce or cultivate or unearth an unlimited supply of Canada Dry Ginger Ale. Followers and others believe The Girl somehow extracts full cans, bottles, and even trucks full of Canada Dry Ginger Ale straight out of the ground. First reported occurrences took place in 2013, when a film crew captured The Girl (who was working at a ginger ale stand that may have been constructed by the Texas-based Dr Pepper Snapple Group, the third largest soda manufacturer in the world and the owner of the Canada Dry brand) dealing with a mysterious influx of customers by extracting fully manufactured bottles of Canada Dry Ginger Ale directly from of the ground. The resulting commercial and an article on popular website Gawker caused a global stir, and pilgrims began flocking to the isolated location soon after. In 2016, the Centers for Disease Control conducted a study that determined that while the average site resident, known as the Ginger People, had gained an average of 135 pounds, none of them showed any signs of those diseases most commonly associated with obesity. In 2017, the group was classified as a cult by the FBI, and the Dr Pepper Snapple Group officially cut all ties and financial support for the area. In 2018, the space was declared a disaster zone by Florida Governor Jenna Bush, and the Federal Emergency Management Administration moved in to supply running water and hygienic plumbing facilities for site residents. Despite mass demand and government interest, no scientific tests have been conducted on The Girl, who is purported to be immune to the aging process, and who the faithful believe still manages the day-to-day cultivation of the area's soda crops.

Status: Undetermined

•

Excerpt from Us Weekly: "Taylor Swift Spurned by Canada Dry Girl"

...But Swift got more than she bargained for when she stopped by the infamous Canada Dry Central Florida "Ginger People" Plantation for a long-rumored meeting with the mysterious "Canada Dry Ginger Ale Girl." The Girl has long been believed to be the subject of the Swift-penned song "Miracles in the Sun."

The Girl, a controversial figure who has been reported to be, in actuality, as many as twenty hired actresses working on a set fashioned by George Lucas' Industrial Light and Magic, reportedly paid no attention whatsoever to T Swizzle's slow burn in the Central Florida shade, preferring to spend her time, as always, feeding her flock of soda worshippers without so much as a glance toward the Swift delegation.

At 2:42, a full three hours after arrival, the blond hitmaker tweeted: "Some people are ruuuuude!" At 2:45, her caravan of tour buses was reportedly back on the road and headed for Jacksonville, where she wowed fans with a sold-out concert that featured her usual bevy of chart-toppers and choreographed dance numbers. She did not sing "Miracles in the Sun."

•

Excerpt from unreleased documentary, "The Canada Dry Girl," Central Florida, 2013.

Carrie Newgent, 29 years of age, 248 lbs.

People ask why we stay. They make fun. I know that. People think we don't know but we do. Yeah we live in a field, but we have the Internet. We have cell phones. Now that FEMA's been out here we have showers, toilets.

Here's what else: I haven't spent a dollar in twelve years. I don't have a bank account. A mortgage. I have a tent and a cot and a sleeping bag and three bottles of Canada Dry a day turned up right here out the Central Florida soil.

Yeah I weigh more than three hundred pretty sure. Most of us do, is what they say. But I know for a fact nobody here been sick since the day they came. Ain't nobody died. You think about that and you tell me would you leave.

Nobody died.

More than five thousand of us been here for over twelve years and we all weigh three hundred pounds and not a one of us has died.

Would you leave?

•

Excerpt from unreleased documentary, "The Canada Dry Girl," Central Florida, 2013.

Denise Perez, 24 years of age, 267 lbs.

Interviewer: Do you still like it? I mean, do you still get enjoyment out of it?

DP: Out of what?

Interviewer: The Ginger Ale.

DP: Do I still like the soda? That's like asking do I like air. Do I like oxygen. Breathing. Shit yeah, I still like it. It's just that here, living like we do, I mean, I just don't have to think about it anymore.

•

Excerpt from "Centers for Disease Control: Obesity in Central Florida," February 2019.

Wes Urban, 32 years of age, 298 lbs.

Once you seen a girl, and this is a little girl we're talking about, pull a truck out of the ground from a ginger plant. Once you seen that you can't go back to your normal life how it was before.

The same people tell me Jesus turned water into wine will stand right there and tell me to my face what The Girl did ain't holy. Relatives of mine done it, standing right where you are now. How come she ain't aged a lick, I ask them, in over ten years? How come I'm still standing here ain't ate nothing but Canada Dry those same years? They can't answer me.

Can you?

Miller Lite

The Hound

I never should have said anything. What happened the night before… it wasn't the first time. It was the first time sober. For him. For me, well, I've known who I am for a long time.

We were taking shots at the bar before the bar, pre-gaming, game-facing. We did a round of jaeger bombs and Fixer knocked some dap and went outside for a smoke. Only when he's drinking, like that makes a difference. I turned to Easy and tried to be cool about it, like, "you know what you're doing later?" Like, "if you wanna come by and play some Call of Duty, that would be cool."

He was tweeting something about the Jets game and he paused, just for a second. Then he finished the tweet and hit send. He turned to the bar and waved for another round.

"Easy," I said. "Don't be like this, man."

Fixer came back in, holding his cell and smelling like Parliament Lights. "'Sup?" he said. He gave me that look like he was disappointed. He checked Easy. He knew what was going on.

"Let's take shots," Easy said. "Let's get fucked up and meet some ladies." He looked at me when he said *ladies*, drew it out, something in his face like a door closing.

I took all three jaegers and did each of them, one by one.

"Really?" Fixer said.

"Let's get fucked up, bros," I said. I took out my credit card and put it on the bar, nodded at the tender. "Meet some laaaaadies." I looked right at Easy.

Right then this guy comes in—big, good looking. Not the kind of guy I usually go for, but you know, the kind of guy who takes up some space, the kind people notice. He's got this girl with him—skanky, Italian, kind of looks like Sammi from *Jersey Shore*. The guy goes off to the bathroom and right away Easy grabs two Lites off the bar and I know what he's going to do and, worst of all, I know why.

Mr. Easy

You know the minute you see him with those puppy dog eyes that you're going to have to do something about it. Something that tells him the score, once and for all. You might fool around a little bit with whoever, and last night was… interesting. And Hound is a good looking dude and fun to hang out with. But god, if only he didn't take it all so seriously. Why does every kiss, every blow job, have to fucking *mean* something? Have to mean everything? You're twenty-five and making money and living in the greatest city in the world and it is definitely not going to last forever. Why can't you just have a little fucking fun?

You're twenty-five but you have plans and those plans don't include somebody like Hound. Those plans have been laid out since you were a teenager. Easy men are Harvard men. They work on Wall Street. They marry women, drive Mercedes, go to church twice a week, and live in Manhattan until they marry, when they move to Greenwich. They have beach houses in Nantucket. Not Fire Island.

What did they say on that old show? Not that there's anything wrong with that. Nothing wrong with that for Hound, and no reason you can't hang out. Shit, it even helps with the ladies to have a gay guy around. Shows how sensitive you are. How progressive. More than once, you've hooked up with a girl who started out talking to Hound.

But Hound needs to know: no matter what happened last night, you're straight. There is a plan, and Hound is not in it.

Hound starts taking shots, like getting shit-faced is the answer, and before he can get any more wrong ideas, you see your opening: big guy heading to the bathroom, hot girl on her own. You grab some Lites and you head on over. Even if it means getting your ass kicked again, it's worth it. This is a message that has to be sent.

The Fixer

Fixer knew this was going to happen. Hound, always leading with his heart. Easy, set on his path the minute he was born. The two of them are like romantic foils in a made for TV Shakespeare adaptation for tweens. Of course this is where it was all going to end up, this little soap opera the two of them have been running for the past few months: all three of them getting their asses kicked in some shithole Brooklyn bar.

He watches them now. Hound making his sad eyes and Easy overcompensating with some Jersey girl at the bar. Trying to make a point. Making it in the dumbest, most obvious possible way, and with Fixer's own beer, no less. Can't he just choose a sexuality and stick with it? And if he's going to experiment, why do that with Hound, of all people? At the very least, they could play more sophisticated games with each other, make this a little more *Dangerous Liaisons* and less *Two and a Half Men*. He realizes that if this is *Two and a Half Men*, that makes him the kid. He will take it.

This will end the way it always ends: Fixer smoothing it over for all of them, hoping they can get drunk enough to forget it before somebody says something he's going to regret. Before somebody says something real.

And right on cue, here comes the boyfriend. Of course, Easy couldn't just hit on anybody. He had to hit on the one girl who came here with a guy. A big guy. The guy goes to the bathroom—the bathroom? —and Easy is there with a beer, hoping to get his ass kicked so Hound can stop feeling sorry for himself and start feeling sorry for Easy. Fixer watches it all go down and shakes his head. Maybe he should move back to Philly, he thinks. But no, everybody there is married already, working on children, talking about 401ks and fucking yardwork. These two are idiots, but at least they are his idiots. He signals the bartender: five Miller Lites.

Samsung

MARCH 18, 2013:

Bam! Posting this from new gig as a Junior Creative Developer and Aesthetic Management Contributor at Meta Games, Inc. So what will I be doing? Oh, just working on a little game called Unicorn Apocalypse. UNICORN APOCALYPSE, BITCHES! This game is gonna be some next level shit. Angry Birds plus Gears of War times Minecraft with some special sauce thrown in just because. Unicorn Apocalypse!

All right, they're calling me in for orientation. More later, suckas.

TAGS: Job, new gig, Unicorn Apocalypse, UNICORNAPOC-ALYPSE!, myjobisbetterthanyourjob

MARCH 19, 2013:

Day two and getting settled in. First of all, our offices are fucking sweet. They look like the set of a sitcom about startups in the Nineties: all glass, brick, big open spaces, these awesome red chairs that kind of look like old diner chairs, but old diner chairs in goddamn space. There's a nap room and a Pac Man and a mini basketball court and free soda and a massage therapist. Massage therapist! I don't even know what that is but I know it's awesome and I have one at work and you don't.

One thing I know: this sure as hell isn't Epic Games, where if you remember, I did my internship last summer, and I thought was awesome until I walked into this place. You'd think it would be all bro-ing down and crunching code, but those guys were more like accountants than anything else, all bottom line and Dockers and project management software (hey Basecamp: suck it!) and timetracking and fourth quarter projections.

I'm going to learn so much from these dudes. Meta rules!

TAGS: Job, new gig, suck it Epic, suck it google, Idranksevensodastodayforfree, MetaGamesRulez.

MARCH 21, 2013:

Free shit, y'all! They gave us all Samsung Galaxies and those sweet mini-tablets yesterday. The guys who are in charge—the one is Asian and old, like maybe 30, and wears this sweater, and the other one is kind of nerdy looking and young and has this Michael Cera hoodie thing happening—got up and were like, new phone policy: now you can use whatever phone you want at work. At first I was like, um, that's the same policy from everywhere, all the time, so like not even a policy at all, really. Then they started handing out these Galaxies and I was like, cool. I mean, I can't really develop on those things but I'm sure I'll get my computer soon and in the meantime: free shit!

20 days til launch!

MARCH 25, 2013:

I sit near this dude named Salvatore who looks like a stand-in for Zack Galifianakis. I have no idea what the dude does but he's hilarious and he rocks this major beard, so I assumed he was a developer. I asked about getting my dev environment set up and he was like, dev what? Then he gave me a high five and was like, Unicorn Apocalypse is gonna be our best game yet! Then I asked about languages and he said he had a little French and said something about MyMotivation. Which I'm guessing is their version of Basecamp?

MARCH 28, 2013:

It's 12 days to launch and I haven't written a line of code for UA. I don't know what's going on around here. Yesterday we had another one of these meetings where the Asian guy stands up and talks a lot about how awesome Unicorn is going to be, and everybody was poking away at Evernote on their Samsungs, and we all got totally stoked about Unicorn, but then at the end the Asian guy just kind of wandered away checking his phone, and everybody else went over to the nap room or to play the Pac Man or they sat at their desks playing Angry Birds on those new mini-tablets with the stylus like the old Blackberries. Research? I don't know.

TAGS: Samsung, Samsung Note, Unicornlaunch?

APRIL 1, 2013:
There's some old lady who works here. I don't know what she does—I think something with the money. But yesterday they tried to give her one of those sweet Samsungs and she's like, I have a system, like a work phone and my personal phone and never the twain shall meet. And everybody is looking at her, like, come on, crazy old lady, that's not how it works anymore. And she's like, respect the system. And everybody was like, thank goodness she's doing the money and not actually working on Unicorn Apocalypse, because: duh.

TAGS: respectthesystemhaha.

APRIL 4, 2013:
Today was a little weird. They keep on talking about this game but not the way I thought we'd be talking about it. Like, I thought there would be writers? I guess I've been thinking about Gears of War, since Sal plays it like all the time. Like at Epic, all these writers were always cornered off in conference rooms banging away at laptops. Like dudes

who had written books, supposedly. Real dudes.

And the process. Holy shit. You couldn't do a thing before a writer finished a script, an editor approved the copy, a continuity tech reviewed the sets and the costumes, a developer approved the code, and then at least two devs had to approve that code for it to get committed, and on and on and on.

These guys are more nimble, I guess? It's just like four dudes in a room talking about what will happen in Unicorn Apocalypse. Like, will the unicorn's horn shoot glitter, or what color is the unicorn's blood?

These guys definitely know what they're doing, though. The Asian guy stands up and talks to everybody a lot and he's really good at it. I guess he's the CEO or something. Or maybe the Creative Director. He's kind of obsessed with the phones, though, so maybe the CTO?

TAGS: GearsofWar, Samsung, unicornblood, unicornsparkle, unicornapocalypse

APRIL 5, 2013:

I was supposed to get paid yesterday and there must have been some kind of thing with the bank or something, or the direct deposit, because, well, no cash. I went to see the money lady with her two cell phones and she was just like, Respect the system, and I was like, Much respect but I need some money here, too. And she just said something about how we were all lucky to be working on a game as awesome as Unicorn Apocalypse, except she called it Rainbow Meltdown. And I was like, Was that your last game that you guys worked on? And she was like, I haven't done improv for a while but yes, I will check on your check.

TAGS: donotrespectthesystem, RainbowMeltdown

APRIL 6, 2013:

There's one dude I swear I recognize. He looks just like one of those guys from the Big Bang Theory, except he's not That Guy. I kept on asking him if we went to school together, if he was maybe one of Dorothea's friends, or if he had ever lived in Ocean City.

Finally, I'm watching TV last night and this commercial for McDonald's comes on and holy shit, there's the guy. Then later on, this other commercial for Budweiser comes on and there he is again, hanging out with a bunch of his bros and drinking Bud Light and hiding from some super hot chick who is supposed to be his girlfriend.

So today I'm like, I totally know where I know you from and I tell him and he's like, I think you're making a mistake, and I'm like, Bro that's totally you, and he just pulls out his Samsung Galaxy and starts typing and kind of scurries away toward the nap room.

TAGS: McDonald's, BudLight, commercialdude

APRIL 7, 2013:

There's still no writers around here and I haven't even seen any code, any QA, anybody, like, playing Unicorn Apocalypse.

I'm starting to wonder what's up. Today I asked Sal what other games he worked on, if it's always like this, if they maybe outsourced dev to India, but he just held his hand up for a high five and shouted UNICORN APOCALYPSE and asked if I figured out to how to do Netflix on my Samsung Galaxy 3.

TAGS: confused

APRIL 9, 2013:

Well, that's it. I'm shitcanned. I'm writing this from the bathroom, but I know they're gonna come soon to get my sweet Samsung Galaxy. We got in today and there were streamers all over the place, these noisemaker machines, a barista and a guy set up in the corner making omelettes to order. I went up to Sal and was like, what's up with all this? And he was like, dude it's launch day.

I was like, So they did outsource to India then? And Sal is like, Dude, just go get a latte and don't worry about it, we're going to happy hour later on.

I go in to see Asian Guy and Michael Cera guy because last time Asian Guy was standing up giving a speech he was like, You can come to my office any time. So I knock on the door and I can hear music in there, and people talking. I knock again and the talking stops. One more time and the music stops. I just stood there, listening. Outside, people were moving around, eating donuts, lining up for lattes, giving high fives and talking about happy hour. They were updating their statuses on their Samsung Galaxies.

I stood there for a while, waiting for something to happen, trying to think about whether I had ever seen anybody do anything on Unicorn Apocalypse, or if it was just in those meetings, that big picture of the unicorn they had all over the office.

They turned the lights out in Asian Guy's office. Outside, people were counting down: five, four, three, two, one....

Then I tweeted at the Epic Games account: "@epicgames I think I quit." I stuck the phone in my pocket then felt it vibrate a response: "@jaymakesgames23 Thanks for your message. Look for Unicorn Apocalypse coming any day now! Enjoy your Samsung Galaxy. UNICORN APOCALYPSE!"

TAGS: Unicorn Apocalypse?

Subway

The first thing was, everybody's voices changed. Not changed deeper, like puberty. This was changing back: they went high, squeaky, like we were seven years old again. This is right after we all started eating the sandwiches. This is when the shit went down.

Fitzgerald from HR was the first to go high. He came back from lunch waving six inches of a twelve-inch Tuscan Chicken around: "free subs at the Subway in the lobby, suckers!" he shouted. Only it didn't come out in his usual smoker's rasp: it came out munchkin, like he was being over-dubbed by a first grader.

We laughed, of course. Only the laugh wasn't normal, either. The guffaws were replaced with tee-hees, the usual roar a shrill tinkle.

"Wait. What's happening?" said Brown from Research. Her husky alto had turned soprano. She gasped, grabbed her neck. She whispered some-thing to herself, then sprinted toward the ladies room.

We all started talking at once. It was the same for everybody: squeaky, high-pitched.

"What the fuck?" Sanders from Creative said. "This is fucking crazy. I have a fucking presentation this afternoon."

He was right. It was crazy. And the rest of us

were no better off. But the sound of his shrieky little voice shouting "fuck," the look of it coming out his mouth—goateed, grizzled, a mouth out of which we had heard the phrases "user experience" and "new paradigm" and "value proposition" hundreds of times in thousands of meetings—it was too much. We giggled and punched each other in the arm. We rolled on the floor, choked on our own high-pitched laughter. Benton from Programming pissed his pants, stood up and showed us all the dark stain, and we went even crazier.

We could feel our inhibitions lowering, even if we couldn't find the word "inhibitions" any more.

"I feel silly!" Benner from Accounts shouted. He picked up a ream of paper and threw it in the air, waved his mouse around like a lasso.

"I *am* silly!" said Claypool from the VP's office. She pulled her dress over her head and ran straight into the wall. She stayed on the floor and giggled.

First we went for the candy. There was a bowl on Selinger's desk, but when we got there, she was sitting on the floor, surrounded by wrappers. She was Sharpeeing pictures of suns and clowns on the scuff-free carpeting.

We had all had those sandwiches for lunch.

The pretty girls were the first to figure out how to make it work. They teamed up in groups of two or three, roamed the office for candy or stray sandwiches, preyed on the nerds. They found Sanders chewing on a twelve-inch Cold Cut Combo and watching Thomas the Tank Engine videos on his computer. "Hey Sanders," they said. They grouped close together, touched each other on the wrist. "What are you going to eat for lunch?" they asked.

He smiled. "Well…" he said, squeezing his Cold Cut. Thomas entered a tunnel and his screen went dark.

"We're going to have lunch together," the pretty girls said. They looked at each other, looked at Sanders, at his Cold Cut Combo. There was something happening but Sanders didn't know what it was anymore. He adjusted his underwear. His face went red. He handed the sandwich over and turned back to the computer. "Thomas is a useful engine," he said.

They ate the sandwich right there, in front of him, in front of all of us, then marched toward Creative to find more stragglers.

Russell from Fulfillment found a spinny chair and we took turns racing one another across the floor, spinning and pushing, five or six of us at once: push spin giggle, push spin giggle.

Then we found the elevators. "So many buttons!" said Kenner from Web Development.

Bailey from Accounting jumped up and slapped the floor number. "And they light up!"

We rode up and down, up and down. Sometimes, people on other floors got on. We were suspicious of these new people. They looked like grown-ups, like teachers or principals, mommies or daddies. But when they opened their mouths to shout "up up up!" or ask if we knew if there was any candy in the building, we knew that they had eaten the sandwiches, too.

Somebody said they remembered there was candy at the front desk of the insurance company on the 11th floor. We found the insurance people in their break room. They had these giant sandwiches—long as a person, cut into little sections. That was the first time we realized how hungry we were for more sandwiches. An Italian BMT or Black Forest Ham or even a Veggie Deluxe. We were starving.

Our pretty girls talked to their nerds. "Hey," they said, "we were going to have lunch together." They looked at the big sandwich like it was a ring or a promise. They touched each other's wrists, smiled their smiles. We stood behind them, skittered and hopped from one foot to the other like we had to go to the bathroom. Those sandwiches were huge, and we were very, very hungry.

Their pretty girls didn't like that. "What class are you from?" they said. "What are you doing here? These are our nerds. These are our sandwiches." They stood up, pointed fingers at our pretty girls.

We backed toward the elevators. The insurance people weren't nice. They should get in trouble, we thought, but there weren't any teachers or principals or mommies or daddies to tell. We wanted those sandwiches. It wasn't fair.

Felker from Security was kind of loitering around near the back. He had either been an Eagle Scout or a criminal. We were never sure which, and it changed, depending on who you talked to. He walked up, casual-like, took a pen out of his pocket, and jammed it in the throat of the first insurance nerd he came across. The guy screamed. Blood poured onto his white shirt. We giggled. Felker hopped up and down. He high-fived the pretty girls, punched the next insurance guy in the face, then walked around the rest of the conference room, tipping over chairs. We grabbed sandwiches and stuffed them in our mouths, put them in our pockets. The pretty girls took the person-long trays and we ran for the elevators.

In the elevator, we ate all the sandwiches. We hit all the buttons. Royce from Advertising peed in the corner and we giggled.

"Hey," one of the pretty girls said. "I know where there's candy. It's in the mall down the street. Candy. Sandwiches. Lots of nerds."

We checked the pens in our pockets. "Let's go," Felker said. The elevator opened and we got off.

Range Rover

Captain's Log: Captain Richard L. Hiltonshire, HMS Evoque, North Carolina Coast. May 12, 1801

The Coast is in sight. America, I pray, although with all that has gone astray on this cursed Expedition, we may just as likely be drifting, rudderless and under power of neither sail nor row, in the shadow of the Dark Continent or astride the Sandwich Islands. This journey has tested reason, and I vow on the sweet Figurehead of Jenny Lind herself, what sits atop the prow of the Ship Evoque, that if through some miracle of our Lord and Savior I am again to step on solid Ground, there I will remain for the number of my days. Let it be testament to our Troubles that I know not another Man aboard the Evoque who has not, in silence or aloud, uttered this very same vow.

Of Men we are down to Twenty-one from our original Seventy-five. Of these, at last count only Eight have been spared of the Bleeding. The afflicted Thirteen are locked in the Hold. This is cruel, certainly, but the only way I can fathom to protect the Health of the remaining. Though I watch its encroaching clouds with great foreboding, I also pray that the coming Squall drowns out the screams of the stricken.

Rich Hilton checked in at Dancing Turtle Coffee, Cape Hatteras, NC, 10:30 AM, May 12, 2013

Oh, new Barista chick: your so hot, but a ca-pachino isn't a latte! Trying to kill me with all this milk LOL.

Awesome waves, today, brahs. Best swells of the week. Sweet way to start a sweet day.

Captain's Log: Captain Richard L. Hiltonshire, HMS Evoque, North Carolina Coast. May 12, 1801

First Mate Saunders estimates we are two miles off shore. If the current remains steadfast and the wind holds, we may just make it to land, but the Weather is not promising and the Journey thus far has, I fear, taught us to expect the Worst while aboard the Evoque.

Behind us, the sky turns pewter and Saunders fears the wind is turning, moving coastward. Bobbing on this angry sea, I am reminded how little control we have over the events of our lives. I should like to attend Church again. I should like many Things. Surely the Good Lord intends every act for a Reason, but after the things I have seen, the blood, the Bleeding…

After the things I have done, I do not know why I have been spared of the Bleeding. The squall from the East grows heavier and I have consigned two more men, anguished and terrified and commencing to bleed from the face, to meet the sure fate of the Hold, and I ponder if the Purpose for my Deliverance has in actuality been Punishment all along.

Rich Hilton pinned MARITIME HAND CARVED SHIP'S FIGUREHEAD, SHIPWRECK DIVE FIND OFF NORTH CAROLINA COAST to the board Awesome Shit I Want.

Psyched! Will go awesome with the stuff I inherited from the old man: aka "Angry Captain Guy" painting and "old boat shit I can't get off the walls without messing up but is probably worth some serious coin."

Captain's Log: Captain Richard L. Hiltonshire, HMS Evoque, North Carolina Coast. May 12, 1801

The storm is upon us. Squall and high winds. Waves as tall as five men. The winds push the old Evoque like driftwood back toward the route of our disastrous Crossing. The Bleeding has started now in First Mate Saunders. I have declined to send him into the Hold. He is a brave and good man and we have traveled many Miles and many Seas together. Our fate seems sealed.

Rich Hilton @surfrichsurfbrah

Anybody know how to get Siri synced up with the Bluetooth voice control in my new Range Rover Evoque? Running late!

Rich Hilton @surfrichsurfbrah

When salesdude demod it looked SO EASY and it's SO HARD. UGGGGHHHHH! SIRI, KILL ME NOW!

Captain's Log: Captain Richard L. Hiltonshire, HMS Evoque, North Carolina Coast. May 12, 1801

Strong Gales and Heavy Squalls. The Evoque pitches about like a twig in a stream. Our sextant is useless in this dark. Our charts have long since been abandoned. I can barely hold the pen as I write. Our Figure Head, the lovely Jenny Lind, maid of our Prow, who was to bring us such Luck, is shaken loose by the Storm. She bobs in the waves, rises up as if to tease us, sinks away with each massive swell.

I have opened the Hold and the few Men who remain Alive have returned to the Deck. The last noble act, perhaps, of a failed Captain beset on all sides by only the worst that Fate could deliver.

I pray for a quick Ending for the rest of us aboard. I pray for whoever finds us here, our bodies, our blood, that they have safer passage…

Rich Hilton checked in at Coastal Coin and Collectibles, Hatteras, NC, 4:20 PM.

OMG I hate Ocean Highway. Took forever to get here and Siri still not synced with the Bluetooth. GRRRR. Worth it? We'll see…

Captain's Log: Captain Richard L. Hiltonshire, HMS Evoque, North Carolina Coast. May 12, 1801

God help us.

Rich Hilton has posted a photo to Facebook, 7:35 PM, May 12, 2013.

Sweet!

Super Bowl

Guildenstern flips the coin and holds it out for Rosencrantz to see.

"Heads," Rosencrantz says. "Again heads." He turns around. "So we were sent for?"

Guildenstern flips the coin. "I hear something," he says. "Music?"

"What do you remember?" Rosencrantz says. "About how we got here, I mean."

"Spanish music," Guildenstern says. "People. A party."

"This place," Rosencrantz says. "Look at it. There's almost nothing here. I mean there's no... visible character to it at all."

"Do you hear them?" Guildenstern says. "The people? The Spanish?"

"I remember places," Rosencrantz says. "Places with more to them, you know? More place to them. Grass or walls. Ceilings. I remember ceilings. Floors. This place...."

"Well there is a floor," Guildenstern says. "And the music. The people. It's getting louder. That's a kind of visible character, isn't it, though?" He flips the coin toward Rosencrantz. The sounds get louder. Music. Chatter as if a party is happening in the room next to them.

"Well it's not visible yet, is it?" Rosencrantz says. And then, "heads."

The music gets louder, as if somebody has twisted a volume knob to full blast. A man enters. He is old, with a shock of white hair. He is wearing suspenders and a sweater. Behind him, another old man, this one African American, with large glasses. Two women follow, both matronly, with white hair and church dresses. They walk slowly, each of them carrying a white takeout bag with Taco Bell written on the side.

"I say," Guildenstern says. "Who are you? Are you who we're waiting for then?"

The white-haired man stops, pulls a taco from the bag, and eats it in two bites. He wipes his mouth.

"Are you the people who sent for us?" Guildenstern says.

"Can you make the music lower?" Rosencrantz says.

"Esta noche, somos jóvenes," the man says. He reaches his hands out for a high-five and the other man stretches, groans, and taps his fingers. The white-haired man gestures, and the group continues on.

"Where are you going?" Guildenstern says. "Can we have some of those tacos? We don't know how long we're going to be here."

"I told you they were Spanish," Rosencrantz says.

"Are you hungry?" Guildenstern says. "Do you think we were hungry all along, then?"

Rosencrantz flips the coin. "Heads," he says.

"Do you think they'll come back," Guildenstern says. "Do you think they were sent for, too?"

"I rather liked the music," Rosencrantz says. "It was catchy. I don't understand Spanish, but I felt like I knew that song anyway. Do you think that's because of this place, because of where we are? Because everything is a little like that now, isn't it? Familiar and then at the same time, not?" He flips the coin, looks at it, nods.

"Do you hear that?" Guildenstern says. "Footsteps."

Rosencrantz takes off his shoes and then his socks. He examines his toes. "They need cutting," he says. "But didn't I just do that? It seems like I just did that. It seems like every time I look at them, they need cutting. Do you remember me cutting them before?"

Two women appear, a blond and a brunette, both very beautiful. The brunette is wearing a skin-tight racing uniform and the blond a pink dress. They move confidently. A chubby man with glasses and very white skin follows. He is less confident, lingering in their periphery.

"Do you speak English?" Guildenstern says. "Are you they who sent for us?"

The blond approaches Guildenstern. She walks right up to him and rubs her chest against his, squeezes his backside. She kisses him passionately, her tongue exploring his mouth. The kiss continues, the only sound smacking, sucking lips. She pulls back, shimmies briefly, her body pushing against his, and then continues walking.

Guildenstern is frozen in place. Rosencrantz drops the quarter and it bounces across the floor.

"Go to godaddy dot com to find out more," the brunette says. She flicks a finger under Guildenstern's chin.

The women continue walking. "Sorry," the chubby guy says, as he moves past. "They do that all the time."

"What is a go daddy?" Guildenstern shouts after them. "Is that who sent for us? Can you do that again, please? I would very much like to find out more!"

Rosencrantz hovers over the coin. "Heads," he says.

Guildenstern looks toward where the women exited. "Do you think they'll come back?" he says. "The way she said that thing about the go daddy, it's like she was... like she was saying something else. Do you get what I'm talking about?"

Rosencrantz regards his toenails again. "See what I mean?" he says. "It's like every time I look, they need to be cut. Every time."

"It's like she was propositioning us," Guildenstern says. "Do you know what a go daddy is? I think it has something to do with relations."

"Relationships. Spatial relationships. Like this place, like how it seems like we're here and we're not here still."

"Relations like between a man and a woman," Guildenstern says. "I didn't think I was feeling... that way, you know, until..."

"Hey mon!"

They both turn to see a tall man dressed in business attire.

"Ya got to turn that frown upside down, mon!" the man says.

"Are you the one who sent for us, then?" Guildenstern says.

"Get happy, mon!" the man says.

"Is that it, then? That's what we've been sent here to hear. Get happy?" Guildenstern says. "Do you know what a go daddy is?"

The man stands still. His smile is unbroken. In his hand, he holds a set of keys.

"Don't worry 'bout a ting!" the man says. "Everyting gonna be all right!"

"Are we dead?" Guildenstern asks. "Are you dead, too? Is this heaven? Is that what you mean by get happy, don't worry about a thing? Is that why you talk like you do?"

The man smiles. He throws his keys in the air and catches them. He continues walking.

Rosencrantz flips the coin.

Guildenstern stares after the man. He looks to the left, then to the right. "Do you feel like we should go somewhere?" Guildenstern says. "Somewhere else?"

"Isn't that how we got here?" Rosencrantz says.

"No," Guildenstern says. "This would be going somewhere else. So by definition not here."

"But what if we were somewhere else and we thought we wanted to be here?" Rosencrantz says.

"We were sent for," Guildenstern says.

"From somewhere else, though," Rosencrantz says.

"But I think I want to go somewhere with food. And a go daddy to find out more. With happy people," Guildenstern says.

"That's the thing isn't it?" Rosencrantz says. He flips the coin. "Maybe we were trying to find a go daddy and tacos before and that's how we got here."

Suddenly the lights go out. There is silence.

"Now what?" Guildenstern says.

"Heads," says Rosencrantz.